Dedicated to My Family

Stefanie Moir, Curtis Auger and Jorden Moir
Jo-Anne Petersen Moir and Silvano Dukic
Alicia, Rick, and Grandkids Lincoln, Zoe and Hailey Brenner
Andrew and Sarah Norminton

So very proud of you all and thank you
for your wonderful love and support.

Special thanks to great friends:
Brian (Red) & Edie Simmons
Carl (Mr. Bach) Bachellier

In loving memory of
Ed (The Dark Horse) Watson
April 24, 1956 – May 8, 2021
"A little sweetness goes a long, long way"

Foreword

I did not grow up in Dundas. But it has been my home for the past quarter century, and as such I have spent many days at the Town's prized possession: the Driving Park. Rich historical significance combined with dedicated preservation, has made it an attraction most Dundas residents value above all other features of the Valley Town. The old oak tree is, of course, a continual reminder of the importance of this space to every Dundas family.

Poet Steve Moir and I first met when he joined my martial arts club here in Town. We instantly bonded, as we had similar backgrounds in real estate, martial arts, and our love of wordsmithing. We have both spent many a sunny afternoon under that tree putting our dreams to paper.

It is a privilege to congratulate Steve on having his poem, "Oak in the Park" chosen for a plaque in the heart of the Park. Born, raised and careered in Dundas, Steve is as much a symbol of growth, strength and stability, as the majestic tree itself. I know that his words of reflection in the poem are shared by many who have also witnessed progress in the Town in a similar manner.

Dundas is full of creative people; it is a legacy this small village has embraced and encouraged. I know both Steve and I feel privileged to be a part of that growing community of people who live and breathe here, but present our work well beyond its borders.

"The Oak in the Park" plaque will stand as a reminder of that legacy, a historic representation of the tree's longevity amidst constant change; change that includes the unhindered dreams of those of us who call this place home.

Robert J. Morrow, Bestselling Author of "The Security". Dundas ON

Author's Note

Most of the 60+ poems herein were written since 2016, when ***Poems of Love and Light*** was first published. This collection clearly shows the evolution of a Poet. With this manuscript, Wordsmith Press has produced and published over 100 poems by Steven M. Moir. My Mom, the Dark Horse and a few living others would be proud.

A worthwhile legacy is to have generations of grandkids ... dream of pretty pink petals raining down on thee, like pixie dust from the Fairy Tree (or perhaps pretty pink piggy snouts?). May you sit with these verses long after I'm gone and get a sense of who I was / am, as,

written words contain energy.

Many poems were written as lyrics to become (award-winning, top ten, awe-inspiring) songs. ~Smile~. Some are heartfelt cries and a few are just rants, or silly musings. Several poems have uplifting, spiritual or thankful messages. Many speak of the importance of asking Creator for help and focusing on the breath, as in meditation, Tai Chi / Qi Gong.

A few poems / songs (as noted) were joyfully created with Yawasoe (One Who Walks With Creator With Speed). Thank-you Coyote. Son, Jorden penned Homeless Figures.

A number of verses show a peed-off, frustrated poet and reflect on difficult times, especially with Covid-19 compounding stresses of already fractured relationships.

The Oak in the Driving Park plaque is a wonderful good news story in these crazy times. Thanks for the support of Parks Staff, especially Tuna and Hal, Councillor Arlene VanderBeek, Hamilton Air Force Association and Dundas Lions Club.

Thank you for your patience, love and understanding.

Toodles,

Table of Contents

50 Years Later
Ed Watson, "Red" Simmons, Len Carter, Mike Nairn

Oak in the Park

Big, big burly ol' bur Oak
Star-lit November stroll
Leonid moon washes o'er
Your stoic majesty unfolds.

Oak in the Driving Park
Yes, we all know the One
Right there 'bout forever
Big shade for hot sun.

Big, big burly ol' bur Oak
Before horses half-miled 'round
Way before Dundas the Town
or Cootes Paradise was found
Few white-men came 'round.

Oak in the Driving Park
Three centuries, plus many years
Hugged him three times 'round
Fingers stretched tip to tip
And I ain't no small fellow,
'Bout eighteen feet at the hip.

Fireworks, bandshell, summer play
Picnics, parties, running away …
Ten generations of man
Damn lucky you still stand.

Meet you by the big, big tree
We'll skip some school
Wander off with your sweetheart
Find the boys, shoot some pool.

Parkside High start-line
Lived a wee walk away
Wander by Him home every day
Four strong winds, he'll just sway.

Big, big burly ol' bur Oak
You just sway and you stay
Energy torus, breathing well
Heaven as earth strong as hell
O' the stories you could tell …

Saws they have touched you
Wounds make gnarly amends
I behold you with wonder
How branches may extend
Sacred geometry, gravity …
Open arms welcome friends.

Big, big burly ol' bur oak
You're just singing your song
Keep doin' what you been doin'
For so very, very long …

Thankful

Half century friends
Freckles of light
Never gone hungry
Don't have to fight

Wrapped in our stories
Oft times we forget
Smallest of blessings
Please don't you fret

Walk in the rain
Hug a young child
Grandpa, I love you
Makes it all worthwhile

Look 'round right now
Find some little thing
To lighten your spirits
Make your heart sing

The little black puppy
Pulled over to me
Tail was a wagging
Worries set free

Quiet times remember
A song from the past
A long-lost love
Sweet memories recast

Warm pumpkin pie
Great Gramma's recipe
Whip cream piled high
Turkey, stuffing, o' my!

However tough it gets
You just have to breathe
You can get thru this
Believe, just believe.

Be kind to yourself
Get over the "stuff"
Times are a changin'
You're more than enough

So thankful I am
It's all yin and yang
Hope you're smiling
Say "Hi" to the gang.

The Hammer

Come from The Hammer
West of the Bay
Generations here
Born and raised

Eagle, falcon, osprey
Peak and The Falls
Slicing thru Town,
The Giant's Rib calls

Found a happy place
Live, work and play
We greet on the street
Raise our family

Countryside right here
At your finger tips
Old friends drop by
See sailing ships

Fewer lunch buckets
Not so much steel
Strength is people
Hard times often real

Here we found love
At an early age
Didn't know at the time
Had to turn the page

Trekked round this world
Always come back
No place like home
My maple sugar shack

Could go on all day ...
Hey, hey, if you may ...
Check out The Hammer
West of the Bay.

Hamilton, Ontario, Canada

This Song is for Healing

Solitary minstrel atop a red-stone spire
Flute flutters echo, echo off sheer canyon walls
A lonely heart reaching for long lost love ...
Kokopelli calls, surrender self, stand tall
Red rocks resonate Akashic hallowed halls.

Fingers wave, weave a mystical refrain
Fine turquoise Spirit Flute remembers your name
Sedona sun embraces our morning shivers
Dawn's first fire delivers, birdsong, possibility ...
Closed eyes see, eagle, condor soaring as we ...

"This song is for healing", on a raptor's wing
Emerald green chakra touched by feathers of blue
Melodic aura embraces the perfection of you
See thru your sad story, to nature's pure glory
"This song is for healing", Pachamama, your feelings ...

Intention is set, time-space spiral propelled ...
Creator creates, music resonates, elevates your cells
Ancestors embrace us, four directions unite
Mourning doves coo, red-tail screes in flight
A soft, gentle breeze sows soothing insight.

Boynton Vista, Sedona AZ

Unity of Purpose

Margot Roi, Artist and Friend

Unity of Purpose

Strokes of all colour
Festival of light
Palette springs to life
With creative insight

Compelling to view
Cannot look away
Tickling our senses
On this November day

Intersecting vectors
Curiosity piques
Impacts our awareness
With glowing critique

See all the people
Bouquets as well
A landscape of contrast
Vibrant as hell

Bullrushes and grasses
Bright shirts and attire
Keep searching for more
The inspiration, the fire ...

Snapshot of a ripple
Vivid Big City Street
A plague ago
We were more less complete

Diversity mingling
Trapped between
Walk and don't walk
A glistening sheen

Random faces
The stories behind
Everyman's struggles
To be less defined

A light-hearted canvas
Proudly hung on the wall
Statement of our times
A blessed windfall

Celebrating the Artist
She's touched our souls
A lifetime of passion
For whom the bell tolls.

For Margot 2020

Spokes in the Wheel

Spokes in the wheel
of our lives
map the Way.
Rays of light
Choose to
follow or stay.
Blissful hub
spirals in space
Spins, illuminates ...
Highlights pathways
Educates
Search for centre
The oneness within
Awaken darkness
We are all kin
The sacred breath
Journey of souls
Spirit mend Self
Long ago, asked for help
I Am, We Are
Author & shooting star

Mistakes made once
Every journey unique
Every lifetime shown
Each valley and peak
Naturally grown
Love's what we seek
The essence of all
Wish it was easy
Oft times we fall
The nature of Man
Try, try again
Listen to Spirit
Maybe Jesus Christ?
Consider what's real
Meditate, just feel ...
Loves' healing way
Teachers each day
Search for "spokes"
Perchance lend a few,
along the snail-trail
karmic pathway review.

Spiral Walk

Walk the pathway of understanding one step at a time. Be careful where you step and make the same mistake once.

Sixty Frickin' Five

Sixty frickin' five today
Comes as no surprise
What seemed really, really old
Now just my wrinkly disguise

Hope there's lots more time
As parties have to wait
Send an emoji thingamajig
To help me celebrate ...

Can't complain too much
Getting 'round pretty well
Embracing a simpler reality
Where stress can go to hell

Newest senior citizen
Bah, humbug to age I say
Gimme my damn discount
Another Groundhog Day

Happily, newly retired,
Pension may get me thru
But the devil wants it all
While weaving words untrue.

A great ride thus far
Made lots of mistakes
Relationships, challenges
Great friends, heartaches

Smallest things I will enjoy
Poetry, music, your every call
Grandpa full of hugs 'n such
Not yet near the final wall

Walking, Tai Chi, ammolite
Breathing-in a good book
Practice doing nothing
Put some bait on a hook

Covid vaccine, Men on Mars
Stress and fears draw near
Our little piece of Paradise
Flaming memories and tears

Worlds turn on gentle breeze
Or thunderous discrepancies
Trust the heavens, feel for light
End is near for our dire plight

So now a senior statesman
Wisdom bubbles thru this mask
If ever you need a guiding hand
Please, please, please just ask

Crossroads in a karmic stew
Heavenly pathways ahead
Bucket list of things to do
Long before I'm newly dead.

Feb 22, 2021

Synchronicity Vibration

Synchronous realities
Vibration transformation
Transcendental pulse
Frequency resonation
Relax, release, receive
Re-re-verberation
Liminality, DMT
Grandmother Aya
Vine of the soul
Altered states recall
dimensional gates
Holographic freefall.

Life is but a dream ~ ~
"I" sees unclearly,
when thinking of "me".
The temporary ID
Your story, my story
Is all just "Our" story
Time – space continuum
Akashic possibility
Transformation, energy
Red-tailed screes
Sacred geometry
Purging, surrender, shivers
Shadow boxer quivers
Questions from answers
... Humble, you got to
Go down low and humble ...

Humility, humanity
Serenity, serendipity
Done, done, done, ...
Water, Aqua, l'eau
Raven, eagle, condor
Home to hummingbird
I, in a circle of we
You are not alone,
Not alone, not alone ...
Meditate ... breathe ...
Cleanse the crystal
Of your sacred heart.

Visions of truth
Shaman's dream
Master surgeon
Mountain stream
Medicine ceremony
Pachamama, please ...
Exploring realms
Inner consciousness
Psychonaut's ceilings
Intention, perceiving
Intuition, healing
Spiritually glowing
To knowing, icaros, icaros,
Death is life ... life cannot die ...
Our feelings and emotion
Truth that never lies

Coyote

(chorus)
'Yote, 'yote, cayo', coyote
Running as the speed of light
Thru the darkness out of sight
Howling with Creator's might
Weave your magic thru the night

Mirror, mirror, shape-shifter
Lessons knocking to be learned
Direct, reflect, be as wind
Hidden wisdom medicine
Drifter shows life's ironies
How you adapt seamlessly
Crazy cunning, cross my path
Teacher, trickster, make me laugh

'Yote, 'yote, cayo', coyote
Running as the speed of light
Thru the darkness out of sight
Howling with Creator's might
Weave your magic thru the night

Wise fools simplify and trust
Beyond the mask, thru the rust
Nature reveals herself in mist
Potential unexpected twists
Transforming possibility
Deceiving, testing playfully
Coyote howl touch my soul
Consider awareness, now let go ...

(chorus)

Mind trap setbacks, change, adapt
All, yet nothing is attached
'Yote shows what's reaped is sown
Change your story, new road home
Run as wind thru moonlight skies
Coyote wisdom, grounded highs
Perfect perfection, prayer ties
Weep in laughter, dawn is nigh.

(chorus)

with Yawasoe – 2017

Coyote Medicine

Coyote coincided with my light
As red-tailed hawks soared in flight
Questions mirrored to reflect
Illusions of being imperfect
Students ready, teacher appears
Blasé, blah, blah, humble seer
I was too comfortable you see
Talked the talk, but fear ruled
Destined for lost possibility?
Kaboom!
Gentle breeze, 'Yote floats with me
Vibrant, vibrant energy
As Creator Moves with Speed
Yawasoe loves Malina Dawn
Buffalo, eagle, Grandmother's song
Purged vile fears, long overdue tears
You dragged "me" out of myself
Like a dusty book on covered shelf
Coyote train you're right on time
Tattered Agreements, so, so sublime
Deep-rooted emotions hanging on
Down the line they don't belong
Melodies change, a brave new song
Haunting, howling, pierce the moon
Shape-shifter, drifter, silhouette,
Shaman, soothsayer ~ glad we met ...
Fences in cosmic sensibility
Mending rips, karmic debts recede
Shadow dancer shapes infinity
Honour the directions hidden gates
As white sage smoke, wisps of fate
Synchronicity, you and me
Spin 'round with flowing destiny
Stir your swirls of rotting stuff ...
Pages and chapters, a history of me
Fairy tale stories just huff and puff
As coyote roams a family grows
The soil speaks, a drumbeat glows
Spiral smoke whispers sacred time
Sweet child sweats, Inipi rhymes
You are Kokapelli in disguise
Seeking, knowing between the lines
Merlin's magic hypnotize
Bless the water, be the skies
Dancer sing, do silly things
Manifest truth and prophesy
Mystic Akashic possibility
Be as the sacred vines Gypsy
Humble service honours thee
Careful where your whimsy may lead
Pay attention, laugh, love carefully ...
You already know, let it go, just be ...

March 31, 2020

T'was the lightest of drizzles
Eighteen percent grey
Death, crowds and sneezes
Interrupted the play

Our story changed
in the blink of an eye
Cortez of modern
days gone by!

Stay in your homes
We're comfy enough
Prairie-dogging plankers
Seas real and seas rough!

Many die too lonely
Like candles snuffed
Medical tough choices
Enough, enough!!

Black bracelets
The haunting faces
Battlefield resources
The unarmed forces.

A loved ones' aura
Droplets unseen
Well-meaning touch
The dearest unclean

Trip of a lifetime
Sing your death song
Like glitter it sticks
and continues along ...

Many are selfless
Some work for pay
Riding ever onward
Few are at play

COVID-19 – Dundas, ON

Twist One Up

Wadda ya say?
It's now okay
Let's twist one up
and snoop a jay

Little Blue Dream
Gummy Bears too
Girl Guide cookies
Gorilla Glue

Load up the bong
and bobble along
Wadda ya say?
It's now okay

Clouds of e-vapour
Exploding forth
Shatter me timbers
The great white north

M&M candies
Medicate me too
Afghani hash
Just like high schoo'

Government jokers
Taxing the show
Street corners busy
Everyone knows

Look round the bend
For Starsky and Hutch
Old habits die hard
When detained for such

Munchies and Buds
Watch Saturday Night
Wadda ya say?
We're Canadian, eh?

Hummingbird

Pixie dust of energy
Light speed sunrays stirring thee
Wind Dancer shimmer in breeze
Step back, recollect, integrity
Sundown, set down peacefully
Bright Rain beckons quietly

Humming, humming, hummingbird
To the centre of the earth
Messenger between the worlds
Tocha Kachina you're the Sun
Swirling iridescent one, one, one ...

Racer bee between the worlds
Like a wisp, a floating pearl
Beneath your wings a hurricane
Nature, spirit light remain
Seek the scarlet nectar power
Kissing Creator's sacred flower

Humming, humming, hummingbird
To the centre of the earth
Messenger between the words
Besa Flora you're the Sun
Swirling iridescent one, one, one ...

Show us where our sweetness lies
Heal in beauty, purify
The fallen soldier your rebirth
Angel footprints, joyous worth
There you be, chip, chip, beauty
Zigzag, bring rain, enlighten me ...
Hear your song, (blow), already gone

Humming, humming, hummingbird
To the centre of the earth
Messenger between the worlds
Chupa Rosa you're the Sun
Swirling iridescent one, one, one ...

with Yawasoe – 2017

Yin Yang Qi

As a bloodhound follows a scent, snail trails of Qi are woven into the spiralling time-space continuum. Sing your death song and die like a warrior going home. Meditate, and if you are too busy to meditate, you are too busy, period.

My Life Story

Grandmother listened intently
to my story of who I am ...
Grandmother listened intently
to my story of who I am ...
Who I am ...? My life story ...
My Grandma, Pachamama ...

She listened and she listened and she truly heard ...
My Grandma ... Who am I? ... My life story ...
She listened and she listened and she truly heard ...
My Grandma, Pachamama ...

Whereupon, she offered me
A shiny new book and a pencil ...
A brand-new book and a pencil ...
A pencil, a pencil ...

She asked me to write another story ... another story ...
She told me to write another story ...
My Grandma, Pachamama ...
Another story
A fine new story
Another story
A brave new story ...

With Yawasoe – 2017

Miracle and Witness

Miracle and witness ...
Without observer, can it be?
A vision no one sees?
Seeds do not grow carelessly
What will be, will inevitably
Empower cloudless wonderment.
Allow yourself reprieve, believe
Momentum gains, no duality
No slots and folders, inner reality
Do not define or bind your mind
Lest you confine infinity
Here's where we're meant to be
Miracles, mirror our reality
Look closely astral royalty
Right here, right now

In the black lab of my mind
A golden retriever returns time
Gaps in space yet undefined
Infinity, forever, lyrics sublime
Obstacles I created, my crimes
Accountability, responsibility
Not paying attention ain't free
Know that shit happens, water falls
Dyad within your hallowed halls
Black and white just shades of gray
Logistics don't tarnish truth away
Backseat driver take a long hike
Energy, excitement, grounding spike
Mantra, mantra, Creator please
Miracles happen with every breeze

Shadow Boxer Ayahuasca

Good Morning Everyone.
Good Morning, Good Rising to your Spirit.
Good Morning to your Ancestors.
Good Morning to your Journey thus far.
Good Morning, Good Rising ...
Good Morning to your Loved Ones.
To your Guides and Angels, Good Morning, Good Rising...

Shadow Boxer, shadow boxer, don't you dare pick up those gloves
Shadow Boxer, shadow boxer, don't you dare pick up those gloves
Shadow Boxer, shadow boxer, why don't you knock me out with your love? Won't you please give up your love ... (Traditional chant)

You are floating in an ocean and see a book on each side of you, just floating in an ocean. You are a seabird and you fly. You look down to see millions and billions of books. Millions and billions of stories, just floating in an ocean.

Humble, you got to go down low ... and humble...
Humble ... ya gotta go down low ... and humble ...

Polish the crystal of your heart.

Who were you before you had a name? What were you called?

Questions come from your answers.

You've always been in the sun, but perhaps have not communed with it.

Is this what I'm not seeing when I'm thinking ... ?

In one thought a universe is created.

Shadow Boxer Ayahuasca

Water, water, water ...

You gotta dance with the one that brought you.

Relax, release, receive ... I am relaxed, I am calm, we are centered.

Life is a dream. The blueprint happened long before you knew your true nature ...

Karmic boomerang.

Going after the light keeps you from you.
You are the light. Your true nature is nature ...

Done, done, done, done ...

You are Love! Then you said to me, takes one to know one ... and we laughed, and laughed, and laughed ...

I said I too many times in the circle of We. Egregore.

Thank you doesn't need a name.

Feed the dark wolf. If you don't, he will become hungry.
If you don't feed the dark wolf, you will never know yourself.
We all like to feed the white wolf, but if the dark wolf is not fed,
it will keep you from you.

The putrid swamp of "family", the angry abuser gaslighting me.

Out of my face
Leave not a trace
Or shadow place
In my inner space

Rising

Aya this, Aya that
Eye in this, eye of that
Size of this, equals that
Size of that, equals this

Isn't your nature
the Divine Self?
Around the corner,
Grandmother's help

Aya this, Aya that
Eye of this, eye of that
Size of this, equals that
Size of that, equals this

Eagle, condor, hummingbird
Circle, spiral, see me soar ~
Humbly master our
journey thus far ...
Walk all your will,
You'll never get far

Aya this, Aya that
Eye in this, eye in that
Size of this, equals that
Size of that, equals this

Hurricanes have past
Rainbows now
Through the miracles of how
Resonating Mother Earth
Water, water, water, birth
Amazing mists of perfectness

Aya this, Aya that
Eye of this, eye of that
Size of this, equals that
Size of that, equals this

Manifesting Manitou
Round and round, thru and thru
See, hear, feel, be brand new
Good mornin', good rising to You

with Yawasoe – 2017

Tell Me

Tell me I'm wrong
It's the ego and pride
Jealousy, blaming ...
I must look inside ...

Tell me my thinking
Is way off key
A poetic fraudster
Exposed by thee ...

Tell me I'm lower
Vibrationally,
too petty to truly
be in harmony ...

Tell me 'bout love
As kissing my wife
Go hide in my corner
Get out of your sight

Look down and point
Away from yourself
Like you've discovered
dust on my shelf ...

Tell me I'm angry,
Keep taking the shit
Tell me what's right
So just make it fit ...

Not one for drama
Often takes a lot
Rise up your somebody
Undo a bad knot ...

Old puma stretches
Coyote creeps off
Tell me it's over ...
'Nother puff and a cough ...

The Water Song

Cycles of the misty moon
Dreams of running in the forest
How fast can you go? Faster ... faster ...
How far can you leap? Far, far away ...
Let go of the ground. Aho!
Float gently down, or quick as a wink
To a sun-speckled mountain stream
Pure water, free water, we're water
The place in my dream.

Nibii Aqua Eau

Nibii Aqua Eau
Oo ah ay
Nibii Aqua Eau
Oo ah ay
Fill my, sacred soul
Water knows
Mountain stream
Shaman's dream
We are one
Energy ... ...

Nibii Aqua Eau
Oo ah ay
Nibii Aqua Eau
Oo ah ay
Pachamama l'eau
Rain on me
Lovely light
Bless the seed
Mountain stream
Shaman's dream
Ancestors live in me

Nibii Aqua Eau
Oo ah ay
Nibii Aqua Eau
Oo ah ay
Water, water moon
Crystal clear
True my heart
Mountain stream
Shaman's dream
Sparkling ...

Nibii Aqua Eau
Oo ah ay
Nibii Aqua Eau
Oo ah ay
Be infinity
Speak your truth
Mountain stream
Shaman's dream
We are one
Energy
Oo ah ay ... ...
Oo ah ay ... ...
...

A hand drum song for Aqua Nibii Waawaaskone – Sound notes correspond to Chakras "oo" as in due (sacral chakra – D), "ah" as in father (solar plexus chakra – E), "ay" as in play (heart chakra – F)

Sometimes

Sometimes It flows ~
Like a group of old souls
Sometimes It blows
right on by ....

What previously
Was destined to be
You may free choose
From your reality

You may never know
Opportunity passed
Gazing intently
At the bottom of glass

When we are blurry
Wounded and down
Kinda hard to look up
Smile from a frown

Sometimes It's surreal
The pathway to bliss
Sometimes It's vapour
To be sorely missed ...

Sometimes It just fits
Like slippers and mitts
Life lessons abound
Soul mate is found

Sometimes It re-forms
Like a mountain stream
To nourish our children
Fulfilling our dreams

Oft times a struggle
Within and without
How to adore others
When you're in doubt?

Broken hearts retreat
Build fences and gates
Shutter the windows
Keep 'way the fates

Sometimes we wonder ...
Sometimes we fret ...
Sometimes, It finds us ...
Sometimes ...

A Simple Back Scratch

You scratch my back
Only until the very second
it feels just right ...
Then you're done.
I could have reveled in ecstasy,
like a big ol' bear,
but you were done.
... Sigh ...

So many things,
just like above.
Half done.
... Sigh ...

A one-way street
He'll care for himself ...
Like a wrinkled old road map
There will be no choice.
A fine wife would try
to please her good man.
Make him ol' time happy
Now and then.
... Sigh ...

Super Grandma

Super Grandma to the rescue
Big bundle of self-righteous Love
Having witnessed visions of light
Since medicina of the soul
Her perfection can do no wrong
Able to limp 'round tall buildings
Barefoot, in a single day ...
~ Super powers allow her to ~
Suggest strongly what you're to do
When she wants you to do it
Takes your car, or wrecks your truck
And is very busy
Fixing the eagle and condor
Saving the water and the trees
Telling the unenlightened how to serve

She was long ago her husband's lover
Now spiraling in the universe
With Peter Pan and the lost children
As her rock and poet at home
Feels unloved and untouched
Disagreeing simply because she can
She proclaims it is her time,
so, funk you, clean up my mess
In the dark distance a light flickers ...

Thnik About It

Thnik a touch too much

'Bout what other people thnik

I should thnik about

Nite, Nite

*

The

Light in me

In the wee of night

~ Caresses the essence of You ! ~

and we go ... flying ... baby !

Out of sight ..., outa sight ..., outa sight ...

Where to tonight ?

Home

Got a nice home
We love it here
Nothing very fancy
Gets better each year ...

A place to relax
Take a load off ...
To putter with pride
Cozy warm inside

Our own hallowed halls
Personal space
A roof and four walls
Just beyond the rat race ...

Only everyday stresses
Little drama or strife
Helps in our search for
The Meaning of Life ...

A bed to curl into
Escape from the fray
Sleepily set sail,
to a shiny new day

Connect to ground
Four paws, four hands
Changes rain steady
Not forced or fanned.

Surrounded by fam'ly
Crazy uncle Red
The 'ol corn whisky
We help him to bed ...

Reciting our blessings
Humbly with thanks ...
Others less lucky
~ Shiver at food banks ...

A bungalow of bricks
To cradle our bones
Feel we're quite royal
Like castle and throne

Worked hard 'n smart
Flowery maiden and I
Doin' darn, pretty good ...
We try and we try ...

Don't dare disrupt
Our simple routine
Flush only crap
Keep the place clean

Come by for a visit
Don't overstay
This is sacred space
The ol' mans' way ...

The Secret

^
Torus
Torus ...
Yin is to yang
Pure, free Qi
All in all, infinity
3-D becomes sacred,
then “” vibrational “”
geometry ... frequency ...
Secrets of synchronicity
4th dimension of fifteen
Auric rainbows we soon see
6th dimension is possibility
Pure creation, connectivity
Akashic time-space memory
Evolving, star seed continuity
Body, mind, spirituality
Little smile, opportunity ...
Harmony, stability, energy
Gaia, Grandmother Ayah
Sativa of the soul, like a
fine moose hide drum.
Deep, deep heartbeat
Leather etched with love
Totem animals whisper of
Turtle Islands' lessons
Our essence as One
In the Inipi of my soul
Red-tail, wolf, White Buffalo,
Dragonfly, hummingbird
Humbling lessons you sow
Within ... as without a doubt
Fair winds my friend ...
See
Feel
Know
or Imagine ...

Silhouettes

^
See
Feel
Know, or
Imagine ...
no time nor space
Swiss mountain lake
Your happiest place ...
Focus on breath, resonate
Energy, prana, chakra, Qi ...
Flow now as a forest stream ...
Feel vibration “““”” frequency ~~
Just p l a y attention,
but not so seriouslee.
Love the colour green
Rhythm rhymes free ~
My reactivity recedes ...
We appear more clearly
Star seeds, peace, unity
Tesla, Einstein, Haramein
Twenty-twelve Kryon
Dark days of humanity
Survived critical mass
Old souls, new energy ...
Evolve, is what we do!
Connect Earth and Sky
Time erodes matter ...
Youthful prowess recedes
Dense matter recycles
Pure light return to sky ...
Lavender, jasmine, soul tie
Always know I am with you
Whispery cheek kisses
Snail trails of crystal tears
High-pitched union, ringing ears.

Snowy Day Haiku

Frosty loveliness

Haiku on a snowy day

May the deer ticks die.

Melting Into You

Melting into you

Flowing laminar as one

Dream of futures past ...

Yin to Yang

Like Yin is to Yang

Dying forms part of living

Energies reform.

Canadian Poet

In memory of Charles **Thomas "Stompin' Tom"** Connors, OC
(February 9, 1936 – March 6, 2013).

Now that I'm
A Poet
And you prob'ly
Didn't know it.
I'll play Tom's songs
And strum 'em
Back to you

Stompin' Tom
And hockey
My poor Ass
From Dundas
Let's twang 'em up
You can
Sing 'em too

Stompin' Tom
And hockey
My poor Ass
From Dundas
Fancy little lyric
Guitar
Lick right here*

Don Cherry
And Ronnie
A bingo and
A stinko
And another
Dang clang
For you

The guitar
She's a flyin'
So won't cha
Please keep tryin'
Sing all them songs
Then we'll
Have a brawl

Stompin' Tom
And hockey
My poor Ass
From Dundas
And another
Dang clang
For you

(And another dang clang ... x2)
This song ain't over yet !
(And another dang clang ...)
(*"The Old Atlantic Shore")

The Mulberry Street Porchin' Band Song

(intro) Hey Silvano
tell 'em who we are...

(chorus)
Downtown in the Hammer
On Mulberry Street
We all get together
Front porchin' a beat

Silvano and Jo
Hearty hugs and hello
A fine Friday night
To crawl outa sight

Richie on skins,
C'mon in ... (solo)
Guy's 'ol guitar
rockin' a'gin ... (riff)

Hey, my friend Jay,
What shall we play ...? (solo)
Eric will just
blow you away ... (solo)

How 'bout some bass?
Rattle your bones
Rocky does that
With undertones ... (solo)

Everyone's here
All walks of life
Dance in the street
Forget the strife ...

(chorus)

Y'all come back now ya hear ...

To: Jo-Anne Petersen Moir and
Silvano Dukic with Love

Girl Named You

(50 bpm, 4/4, Key C, finger-style outside / inside, arpeggio.

C 5,2,4,3, strum
Hey, I wrote a song
Π V Π V Π
Em 6,2,4,3,5, strum
'Bout a gi-rl named You
Π V Π V Π Π

C 5,2,4,3 strum, strum
Finger-style guitar
Π V Π V Π Π
G/B 6,2,4,3,5, strum
May you never be blue
Π V Π V Π Π
Am 5,1,3,2,4, strum
If only I could sing ...
Π Π V Π V Π
F/C 5,1,3,2,4, strum
Pluck the 'ol guitar strings
Π V Π Π V Π

C 5,2,4,3, strum
Got a second verse
Π V Π V Π
Em 6,2,4,3,5, strum
Not the same as the first
Π V Π V Π Π

C 5,2,4,3, strum, strum
Say it like a po-em
Π V Π V Π Π
G/B 6,2,4,3,5, strum
Cause my singin's much worse
Π V Π V Π Π
Am 5,1,3,2,4, strum
Hey, smile that big, big smile
Π Π V Π V Π
F/C 5,1,3,2,4, strum
Let's hang out for a while
Π V Π Π V Π (solo)

C 5,2,4,3, strum
Girl, a song 'bout You
Π V Π V Π
Em 6,2,4,3,5, strum
Whimsy yet rhapsilly
Π V Π Π V Π

C 5,2,4,3, strum, strum
My fat fingers strum
Π V Π V Π Π
G/B 6,2,4,3,5, strum
The ol' wash-board of chords
Π V Π V Π Π
Am 5,1,3,2,4, strum
Best to keep practising
Π V Π Π V Π
F/C 5,1,3,2,4, strum
If only I could sing ...
Π V Π Π V Π

for Stef,
Very Proud of You

The Jiggly Ol' Belly Fat Blues

How did you
come by that?
Ya know the
Jiggly ol'
Belly fat.

Getting round
Got around
What'cha mean?
Put me down
Pound for pound

Oh hell that
Belly Fat
Plump is me
Curvy see ?
Chun-ky !

Been watchin'
the game
Not playin'
the same
Came up lame.

Gettin' slow
Mojo low
Driftin' snow
Slice a pie
A la mode

Plain to see
Look at Me
Not a frown
I'm Happy
as can be

The jiggly ol'
Belly Fat Blues
Baby maybe
Make that
Ol' time news

Just for today,
Why not say,
Hey, it's quite okay ...
Lovin' that
Belly Fat Blues.

Kaua'i Sunrise

Ringing in the ears
Is always hear
I gaze from
Left to right

Cannonball!!
Soft sunset light
Sparkles my eyes
Kisses my sight

Light beams twirl
Mountain stream
Fluorescent pink,
A purply gleam,

Peachy auras
Tracing with love
The volcanic ridge
High, high above

Cannonball!!
Spritzing to
A luminous
Pastel rainbow

Bleeding to the sea
Beckoning me
To follow thee
The fleeing majesty

The burning surf
Fiery brick road
O'er the edge
Of the earth

Cannonball!!
Last light today
Slack guitars play
Like the old days

Moon beams
o'er Hanalei Bay
End of the road
For another day

Princeville Kaua'i, HI

Live Bait or Lure?

Live bait or lure
Hmmm .... ?
Pure crispy morn
Billowy mist on glass
A soulful cure

Pre-dawn yawns
Coffee drips on
Leave Love a note
"Fillets, sunset, sauté ..."

Shuffle to me boat
Calm waters and mind
Joyous being afloat
Tug on the line ...

The Pick and Choose Blues

Pick 'n choose
Pick 'n choose
Dazed 'n confused
Lazin' round Town
Feel kind'a down
O' won't cha tell me
Just what to do
Decisions, decisions
I'm through !

(chorus)
If you're just not
Sure, what to do
You just might have
Pick and Choose Blues,
You just may have
Pick and Choose Blues

How do ya know
The pathway for you?
Can I help ya
with that, show ya
a thing or two?
Gotta relax
Go with the flow

Take a deep breath
Feel the mojo

Wallet is full
Weekend is here
Wonderin' now
What kind of beer?

Party partakin'
Been there before
My Mama would say
Baby put it away
Wide open yer eyes
Clear up cloudy skies
Get offa yer ass
I can't sympathize

Pickin' a tune
Pick A, B, or C
Throwin' the dice
Roll one for me
Jiven' all day
Dance floor tonight
Noddin' your head
Rock outa sight

Tappin your shoe
Singin' along
Gotta be movin'
Do carry on...

Be-boppin' along
Saturday night
Buddies and I
Ladies look tight
Stumble around
Got in a fight
Bobbin', weaving
Left and a right
Knuckled my noggin
Shiner so bright

O' the choices
Aren't too tough
My life's okay
But the Pick and
Choose Blues ain't
Goin' away
Pick and Choose Blues
Goin' away ...

Special Someone

Special someone
Into your life
What does it mean
To be a wife?

Seasons of change
Lives rearrange
Love's funny thing
Out of the cage

(to be continued)

Paihia, NZ

The Ties

Ties that bind
O' I've done
My time
In the prison
Of my mind

Bars aren't there
Look and see
Break out, run free
Pure energy
Believe in thee

Fly, fly baby bird
All you can be
Soar to great heights
Triumphantly
Fresh new reality

Speak your truth
Own best pal
Ask Spirit to be
guiding thee
And so it shall.

Snip the webs
Fear no black
You're a light source
Send them back
With kind thanks ...

Life's lessons
Hard learned
Got the point
No darkness tonight
Just love'n light

Crystal clear present
Thank you so much
Aura glows bright
Innate eyesight
Infinite delight

Ties that bind
Truth that is
Challenge to be
Fine-tune your mind
Liberate, be free

What's Happening

A lifetime ago
and decades before
the girl I met,
now the woman I know.
The talk, the banter,
the laugh or two.
Became a great
friendship with you.

A time from now
Have a wee chat
"How've we been?"
Do we like it like that?

Seeds we're sowing
Watch them grow
Questions, some answers
Do we need to know?

Strong and wise
Goose bumps for sure
That healing touch
Yet insecure

Communicate
Come talk to me
What's happening?
What's to be?

Fun and caring,
easy times
Friends and family,
making up rhymes
A foxy lady
rings my chimes
I write poems
for her sometimes

Crossroads in life
Paths come and go
The best one to take
Is oft hard to know.

A special person
You never forget
Friendship that grows
Passion and sweat

Take my arm
We proudly stroll
Stairway to Heaven
and a lot of soul.

Interdimensionality

The space between
Neither here nor there
Follow the breath ...
Follow the breath ...
To the feeling,
the raw emotion,
the Essence.
As Rumi sleeps,
we are indeed,
together there.
Love everlasting
Always ...

Past lives or promise
As one in stillness
Surfing time/space
Then upon notice
Gone ...
Like grasping straws
of sacred smoke
A bubble bursts
Fragile pathways
Forgotten for now
Follow the breath ...
Follow the breath ...

Think In Terms Of ...

En er gy

Vi bra tion

Fre quen cy

Pa cha ma ma

Re son ates

With Me

Ea gle, Con dor

Pro phe sy

Campfire Chant – Flute / Drumming

Poem A Day

I'll write you a poem
a day my dear
I'll write you
a poem a day

When you are near,
or far away
I'll write you
a poem a day

Pathways unclear?
To help ease the fear
I'll write you
a poem a day

In my mind you're
crystal clear, as
I write you a poem
a day my dear.

Season Has Ended

Our Season's ended
Goodbye Twin Flame
Lessons we learned
No one to blame

Perhaps when we love
Ourselves some more
A Soul Mate may
Appear at the door

Like a big bald lie
In this beautiful place
Love has long lapsed
Into empty space.

Always on the edge
We just disagree
Doesn't matter what
There's disharmony

Life's lessons learned
Twin Flames burn hot
No time to relax
This fish got caught

I'll see you less
As time goes by
No longer heeding
Your plaintive cry

Season finale tonight
We've lost the fight
A mistaken union
Reflecting no light

Won't appeal any more
For just one last try
Honey, we both know
We're living a lie.

Two Toonies

Got two part-jobs
Two puppy dogs
Two toddlers to please
Low opportunities
Moo-moo, ol' school
Tomorrow's dull tool
Too few taboos today
Inhale green and pray
Tobacco token tomb
Total and dual – ity.

Place's too small
Rent is too, too high
Sometimes, so am I
Like two-steps behind
Tumultuous times
Total three eyes blind.

Got my two-tone
pickup truck towed
today to Toledo.
I'll toot, toot to you
Truly drop on thru
When I tour into
Incognito, to
tooth your tasty
tata stew, with
tubers 'n tomato roux.

Score is two t' two
It's a playoff preview
Boys in blue tutus
Shuck a puck and lose
On toque and toonie
Tuesday in Toronto.

The Bitchin' Baby Blues (2)

Tell ya 'bout my baby
With eyes blue 'o so blue
We were so, so happy
It was really good news
A few short years later
Got The Bitchin' Baby Blues

Cool blue eyes a flashin'
Thinks she can't do no wrong
I just crawl out of sight
Pen to paper this song
That's the pathway I choose
With The Bitchin' Baby Blues

Now I'm tryna do right
Watchin' my P's and Q's
It don't matter none Son
She's got the sights on You
Hopin' there's a potion
For The Bitchin' Baby Blues

'Cause I'm surely no saint
Gotta make my own breaks
Hitchin' to a bitchin'
C'mon for Heaven's sakes
You know I can't break thru
Bye, bye Bitching Baby Blues.

2011 NZ & 2020

Keep It Simple

Some salient stuff
Keep it simple son
Simply, sim-pli-fy
Settle the sunny side
Ask for help ...
Dear Creator ...

Notice the breath
Naturally, in and out
Silent spaces between
Breath is Now
Where we want to be
Our safe harbour
from darker reality.
When you're upside-down,
and inside-out
Focus on the breath
Follow the breath
Freedom is within

The monkey-mind
scatters, we gather
it up, and again ...
focus on the breath
Ask for help ...
Dear Creator ...

Bubbles, bubbles
Boil and burst
Poppity, poppity
Baggage and barriers
Isolate, percolate ...
Reactions, feelings
Impressed old energy
Before a babe's words
Oldest sensations and
aversions rise, resonate,
illuminate, detonate,
Sankhara evaporate.

Pay Attention

Pay attention my teachers would say
One day you will take our place
We may guide with gentle breeze
Or firmly knocking synchronicities
Make these knowings as your own
Let Ancestor messages be sown
Into your fabric, the very marrow...

Grandmother smiles, tribal fires glow
Speak your truth, let Creator's juice flow
One step aside, get out of your way
Observe perfect floes, natural array
Wisps of smoke-like intuity
Trust me, I love you, as grasses sway
Our blankets hug you, let us pray

Earth and fire, heaven and sea,
Won't you please come back to me
Four points bearing clarity
Totem symbols clans connect
Currents of change with respect
Young mind too active, that's ok
Pay attention, a title role you'll play

Chances change as we look away
Missed potential, another lost pay
Pay attention to thoughts and words
Sculpt your person with gentle verbs
Childlike wonder, complete dismay
Every raindrop, every which way
Abuelita Cachoeira*, named this day.

*Grandmother Uprising Waterfalls

'62 Wide-Ass Rambler

One pretty good year
'til the chrome veneer
Fell off you my dear.
Backseat was too near

'62 wide-ass Rambler
O' she's a gambler
With four on the floor
like a trailer-park whore

Muffler needs some care
Exhausts like a cloud
A/C just blows hot air
Horn is mighty loud
Not much to look at,
even with the top down

Left, left, left ...
Sign here, pretty please
Should have known better
The 5-year lemon squeeze

Factory recalls
Warranty expired
Nuts and bolts loosened
Rusty frame retired
Undercarriage revealed
the good deal repealed
Must turn away now,
any-way, any-how!

Burnin' out each day
Was a smokin' ride
Puller out the ditch
by the trailer hitch

Drivin' down the road
Ya, the new car smell
It wore off real quick
Died and went to hell.

Bloody well knew
Glimpses were true
Got the highway shakes
comin' home to you
Should have sped away
like a robber that day

Rev the engine way up
She'll empty your cup
The tank runneth dry
In the junk yard she'll die.

She just stopped purrin'
Dozen years in review
Big, fat ol' cranky Rambler
Wallet guzzler sixty-two

Back seat's unused
She's antique today
Just a piece of history,
along the fuckin' way.

Two Young Sisters

Never had a voice
Growing up defiled
Had little choice
Don't get him riled

Became very quiet
Scared as hell
Father's tantrums
Yell and yell ...

Mom and Dad
Bicker and fight
That's all they knew
It must be right

Ex-husband, boyfriends
Beat her way down
Guys with problems
Welcomed around

She found her voice
Will now disagree
With every single
word from He.

The sky's not blue
You won't boss me
Must work on herself
Emotionally

Because she can
It is her right
If He is there
To scratch a fight.

I am woman
Hear me roar
Not again, please ...
Good man out the door.

Paperclip

... Wake, walk, Tai Chi, meditate, anicca, repeat ... Wake, walk, Tai Chi, meditate, anicca, repeat ... Wake, walk, Tai Chi, meditate, anicca, ...

Stone Cold

I'm cold,
Stone Cold.
Got no feeling ...
Got no home ...
Just got hands,
cold as stone ...

And when I die ...
Lots of secrets,
Tattle told.
That's right ...
Look around
I'm cold,
Stone Cold !!

Bob Loblaw

Bob Loblaw with Matty McGee
Shot Sherriff Schnebly
In the knee, by the tree
But they did not shoot the Deputy
I, Bobby Bailey
See'd McGee shoot Schnebly
In the knee, by the tree
Your honour.

Name a Rainbow

This flu is brand new
It may kill you
Lonely, breathless adieu ...
Goodbye Granddad, Dark Horse too
We'll name a Rainbow after you.

Homeless Figures

There are many Canadians without a home,
They stay about the street;
They sleep and beg and roam and roam,
And have very little to eat.

The government tried to tally the souls
That were without address:
Their census plan had many holes
And was without success.

The result was smaller than predicted;
It was quite far from what studies depicted.
The government needed better ways to count
These people to portray the correct amount.

They tallied the homeless that sought refuge
In the year two thousand and one;
The number of them was just too huge,
So this could not be done.

The winters are harsh and unforgiving;
It affects the way the homeless are living.
A problem like this should come to an end;
Always be kind and a hand you should lend.

By: Jorden Moir, 2002, 15 years old

Elder's Prayer

Breathe deeply young warrior
We see your good heart
Wrapped in the puma of youth
You have much to learn
We have much to impart

Listen deeply young warrior
Believe in your breath
Awaken Creator's light
to infinity within
When all's revealed, One is left.

We were once strong like you
At times you must forgo the coup
Many buffalo now are few
See far beyond distant hills
Feel the seasons, know the land
Bend as saplings, understand?

See seven generations
Ancestors, unborn
Embrace the path, breathe thru fear
Respect yourself and all that grows
Pray to the drumbeat of your heart
Til knowing becomes a part.

Feel the love of white sage seers
We whisper direction in your ears
Flow with winds, four directions unite
Medicine wheel teachings to impart
Cleanse the crystal, your blessed heart

Fire, water, earth and air,
Black as white, please take care ...
Thoughts are actions, sacred life
Nodes and nulls, Gaia energy
Pay attention to senses, just be ...

Chakras like a mountain stream
Feel the oneness, the purity
Rainbow healers of prophesy
Eagle, condor, lighthouse, sea
Shadow boxer masculinity
Pachamama walks with thee ...

Vortex plants medicina ~
Intention, peace, manifest
Challenge your children
Smile, give back gratefully
Ancestor pride shines in thee
Listen humbly ... breathe deeply ...

Christephanie to Sea
(Alex's Song)

Shovel and a pick, and a shovel and a pick
Shovel and a pick, and a shovel and a pick

Put the tools away, goin' sailing on the Bay
Put those tools away, goin' sailing on the Bay

Christephanie to sea, Christephanie to sea
La, la, la, la, la and a la, la, la, la, lee
Christephanie to sea, Christephanie to sea ...
La, la, la, la, la and a la, la, la, la, lee

Sailor sails away, yeah, sailor's sail away ...
Sailor sails away, yeah, sailor's sail away ...

Christephanie to sea, Christephanie to sea ...
Doobie, doobie-doo and a doobie doobie-dee
Christephanie to sea, Christephanie to sea ...
La, la, la, la, la and a la, la, la, la, lee.

The Kiss

Inca Trail behind us
Amber, peach Andes' sunrise
Piercing rays light the Sun Gate first
As they knew it would ...

Intipunku
Overlooking Machu Picchu
At the Gate of the Sun
We stand wearied nearby

Not a cloud in the sky.
Unusual for this place
Stars step back from the light
Awe of breathing in this scene
Defining moment for two lovers

Together forever in The Kiss
Shutter of life, focus and click
In that mystical, magical moment
We are one and true together
A favourite photo remains ...

~ One Last Poem ~

Ed (The Dark Horse) Watson

~ One Last Poem ~
A friend for the ages
My Mother's other Son
Too soon, life changes

Half century best friend
Got your back, wise advice
The Dark Horse remembered
Definition of nice.

Sports, parties, doublin' down
Shortstop triple plays
Howdy doody the clown
All just better, with Eddie around

How did we survive
those formative years?
High Rolling tales to tell
Werewolves, smokes and beers

Strength of fine family
Lynn, Mark, Thomas, Leanne
Continue the legacy
Of this wonderful man

Kings and peasants
Were respected the same
You touched so many lives
They all knew your name

A little sweetness
Went a long, long way
Like father, like son
John guides, let us pray

You were way too early
At heaven's gate
Everyone down here wishes
You were fashionably late

When we enter this place
We say hello to Ed
Snail trails of energy
Greetings, fond memories

Fly with the eagles
The CT-133
A moment of silence
We honour thee

April 24, 1956 – May 8, 2021

Steve & Ed & T-133

ABOUT THE AUTHOR

Steven M. Moir, is attempting to retire and lives in Dundas, Ontario, Canada.

He is a graduate of McMaster University and has pursued an interest in the spiritual, healing and martial arts for many years. Steve plays and teaches Tai Chi / Qi Gong, enjoys meditation, wordsmithing, improving on the guitar, writing music (with help) and the world's great hikes. He creates jewellery with Alberta ammolite and silver (DeerTrailOriginals).

His first published collection of 42 poems entitled **Poems of Love and Light** (available on Amazon or through the Author) was first published in 2016. This was a lifetime ago.

If these words resonated with your assorted senses, I am very pleased.

If you like, please contact Steven at: smoir3@cogeco.ca.

Toodles,

Back Cover

Joseph Chilvers (1890 – 1960) – Great Grandfather

Mayor of Kincardine, ON (1950 & 51)

Mom's most marvellous man & owned the General Store

Mom - Patricia Anne (nee Stewart) Moir, Auliffe

June 7, 1934 – April 12, 2019.

The cute little fellow is Me

1956 - and still chugging along ...

Manufactured by Amazon.ca
Bolton, ON

40126011R00044